Tylorin

Kenneth Haines
Tylorin

Tylorin's Journey

Isbn: 979-8-89569-415-2

Tylorin

Tylorin's Journey

Kenneth Haines

In the fair and fanciful realm of Eldaf, where the air is thick with the promise of adventure and the sweetness of laughter, one finds both elven elegance and human humility side by side. Yet beneath this veneer of camaraderie lies a sorrowful tale; for poverty casts its long shadow, leaving many a soul, particularly those of the graceful elves, to wander the cobbled streets like specters, seeking a nook or cranny to call home, yearning for a scrap of safety in a world that seems dead set against them.

The brutality that humans inflict on elves has been significant, and humans have gained power over the elves' kingdom.

Among the homeless in the ruins of Eldaf, a young elf mother did her best to stay hidden, clutching her child close. The fear of humans discovering and taking her son haunted her every step.

In the shadows of the ruins, a dark figure moved silently, observing the suffering and chaos that had befallen the kingdom. He remained hidden, watching and waiting for the right moment.

That moment came when he saw the young elf mother with her child. He scurried closer, his voice a whisper in the night. "Follow me, but be very quiet and stay close. We must not let the humans see us."

Tylorin Jaean hesitates for a moment, looking around cautiously to make sure no one was watching or was near. She then quickly in a hurry pace and follows him, holding her young son tightly in her arms.

She followed him to a forgotten area in the kingdom; it was overgrown with vines and briars. She watched him slide a panel back and followed him inside. He slid the panel back in place and jammed a long rod so it couldn't be opened.

He led her down into an old mine shaft, where an ancient pumping trolley car sat on the tracks. "Hurry, lay your bundle in the basket," he instructed, quickly removing the rocks that blocked their path. "Okay, help me. Grab the handle, and we must pump it."

At first, the trolley resisted, its mechanisms stiff from years of disuse in the dusty shaft. But as they worked together, the rust began to give way, and soon they were moving, the trolley creaking and groaning as it picked up speed.

Tylorin Jaean and her savior continued to pump the handle, her arms aching as she put all her strength into the effort. She glanced down at her son, who slept peacefully in the basket, unaware of the danger they were fleeing.

After what felt like hours, a dim light appeared ahead. "Is this the end of our tunnel ride? Are we far enough from the kingdom to avoid being found?" The questions weighed heavily on both their minds as they pushed forward, hoping for safety and freedom.

We burst through the end of the tunnel, my grip tight on her arm and the handle. She clung desperately to the basket. Sticks, vines, and old wooden planks flew in all directions as the trolley car crashed through the barrier. We braced for the impact that never came, our hearts pounding as we emerged into the open.

The trolley car picked up speed as it started down an incline. All we could do was hold on to the handle and each other, the fear in both of us growing stronger.

Tylorin Jaean clung tightly to her savior and the handle, her knuckles turning white from the strain. She glanced down at her son, nestled against her chest in the basket, still peacefully asleep.

As they continued to roll, trees and bushes whizzed past them, a blur of green and brown. The fear of what awaited them at the end of the ride loomed large in their minds.

Suddenly, a loud sound enveloped them, and they felt fine sand burning against their faces and hands. A cloud of white obscured their vision. The trolley car came to a halt, and as they disembarked, the dust settled around them, revealing their surroundings.

"Seems we ran into a soft sand pit that was used to stop runaways, and we were thankful for it."

There in front of us lay a green forest, wildlife running free. "Here, let me carry the basket for you. We need to get far away from the tracks, just in case they ever find it back at the kingdom."

Tylorin Jaean nods and carefully hands her savior the basket with her son; then she follows him through the dense forest. She had never been outside the kingdom before and was captivated by the beauty of the scenery around her. She felt the presence of the animals, sensing their curiosity and peace. Unlike humans, elves had the ability to communicate with wildlife, forming a bond that went beyond mere survival.

She felt a sense of awe at the sight of the wildlife

running free and a pang of sadness for her own loss of freedom.

She looks at her savior, carrying the basket, and at her young son, sitting up and looking around curiously.

We rested for a bit, taking in the scenery and catching our breath in the fresh air. Suddenly, I heard something and whispered, "Shush, listen." It sounded like water nearby, and we desperately needed it to survive.

She lifted her son from the basket, letting him stretch and move around a little. I wandered not far away, listening intently. The sound of water grew closer, and I hurried back to get them. "I think I found water," I said, offering to carry her son. She picked up the basket, and we moved forward together, following the sound.

After a few minutes and down a slight incline was a stream. We hurried to the stream, but I told her to wait so I could make sure it was safe to drink. I smelled the water; it didn't have an odor, and I looked around and saw other wildlife drinking from it, so I took a handful first.

"It's safe to drink," she cupped her hand to give her son some water, then she drank some. "We are safe here;

relax and rest, and I will check around for something to shelter us."

Tylorin Jaean sighs in relief as she sits down and gives her son more water. They both are lying near the stream, her son in her lap. She watches me exploring upstream and downstream; she feels grateful for the help and protection I have shown her.

I walked a little away from the stream to what looked like a good spot to build a shelter for the night, but instead, I found something more interesting, and it was a godsend for us.

I hurried back to them and told her to follow me. "Look what I found." I lifted her son onto my hip, and she followed me.

There, behind a thick layer of vines and foliage, was a cave not far from the stream.

We entered and just about could see, but I told her not to disturb the coverage to the cave for fear it could be seen by others; she agreed. "Her eyes widened in surprise and relief as she saw the cave. 'This is perfect,' she whispered, a smile breaking through her exhaustion."

"Inside, the cave was dimly lit, with shadows dancing on the rough stone walls. The ground was uneven but dry, and a small pool of water glistened in the corner, fed by a trickle from the ceiling. There were also boxes and crates along the wall and old furniture strewn around, looking as if people or elves had lived here many years ago."

Tylorin is looking around the cave while I am holding her son against my hip. "Look for anything I can light so we can see better," I asked her. She rummages through the dusty, dirty boxes and crates for something useful. After a few minutes, she comes from the back of the cave holding two torches.

I took the torches from her as she took her son from me. Getting down on the floor, I pulled out my flint and stone. After a few tries, I managed to get a spark, and soon we had light. The flickering flames illuminated the cave, revealing more of what lay around us. I lit the other torch and handed it to her after she had settled her son safely into a basket.

With the cave now better lit, we could see the remnants of a past life scattered about. Old furniture, long abandoned, stood against the walls, and the boxes and crates hinted at stories untold. Tylorin held her torch high, casting long shadows as she moved deeper into the cave, her eyes scanning for anything useful.

Seeing what was around us and knowing we were far from the chaos at the Kingdom, I realized this would have to do for now. We needed a place to rest and gather our strength for the days ahead. Tylorin agreed with a weary nod. "Yes, you are right," she said, her voice heavy with exhaustion. It was clear that both she and I needed time to recoup and rest. It had been a long day trekking through the unknown.

As we were settling down, I took off my cloak and hood, and Tylorin grabbed her son and held him tightly against her chest. In the light of the touches she realized that she has been following a human and not an elf like herself and the fear was coming back and resurface and all the stuff she saw happening to her people flashed through her mind. Holding her son even tightly and moved back away from her savior, her heart racing with anxiety, she looks at her savior with fear and uncertainty, unsure what to do or say.

Her savior stood up and then got down on his knees. "Please don't be afraid of me," he said softly. "I promise you, I would never hurt you or your son. It is my duty to protect you both. I am nothing like the humans back at the Kingdom. What they are doing to your people is wrong, and they will pay for their sins when the time comes."

"When I saw you trying to hide from the humans, I knew it was time to leave. I saved you from the fate of losing your son because I could not bear to see that happen."

Tylorin's fear slowly began to subside as she listened to her savior. She took a deep breath and looked at him, trying to calm herself. Her mind raced with thoughts. She knew what he had done to save her and her child, but she wondered why. What were his intentions?

She moved away from the cave wall and gently lowered her son back into the basket. "I... I'm sorry," she said, her voice still shaky. "It's just... humans have caused so much harm and death to my people. I can't help but be afraid of being with a human. I'm not saying you would harm me—your actions have shown just the opposite."

He nodded, understanding her fear. "Yes, I understand what you saw and went through. I did too. Once I found a way to escape that chaos, I knew I needed to help. When I saw you, I knew I had to step in and get you far away from there."

Tylorin took a deep breath, her fear slowly giving way to a cautious trust. "Thank you," she whispered, her eyes meeting his. "For saving us."

"You're a good person," she said, a small smile forming on her lips. "Not many humans would have the courage to do what you did. You risked your own life and safety to save another, and that's not something to take lightly."

She watched as her savior settled down on the floor, her son crawling from the basket to him. Her son climbed into his lap, and he cuddled the child, kissing his forehead tenderly. Tylorin watched this scene unfold, feeling a mix of emotions: gratitude, relief, and even a hint of affection—feelings she hadn't experienced in a very long time—wash over her.

She knew that her savior had been kind and gentle with both her and her son, and it warmed her heart to see her son so comfortable in his arms. She watched as they lay down, her son cuddled up to him, and they both fell asleep. A feeling of peace washed over her, and she started to feel tired as well. Slowly, she lay down beside her son, the warmth of his small body comforting her. Soon, we were all asleep, the flickering torchlight casting gentle shadows on the cave walls, a temporary sanctuary from the turmoil outside.

A slight noise and I jolted awake, then I saw that they both was in my arms sound asleep, she looked so peaceful cuddled up to her son.

I kissed her son's forehead, then I tenderly kissed hers, I slowly slid my arm from underneath them and covered them with my cloak and quietly I stepped outside into the early morning sun light.

I walked to the stream and put my hand in the water, feeling the coolness. Then, realizing how dusty and dirty I was, I stripped off my remaining clothes and found a deeper spot to lie down and clean off the grime and stinky soot from my body.

As I'm washing off the grime, I can't help but think about the events that led us here. I feel a sense of relief and freedom from being away from the chaos of the kingdom. But now I have a responsibility to her and her son, and I will protect them with my life if I have to.

As I was washing up, I didn't realize her son was watching me and pointing to the water. He came closer, and I took off his dirty rags of clothing, sat him down between my legs, and washed him, getting the grime and soot off his little body.

He is giggling as I dunk his head just enough to get it wet, and with my hands, I scrub his hair to get the soot out of it. He looks up at me with the biggest grin; I don't think he ever had the chance to really wash up.

Tylorin woke up, and fear quickly rose within her as she realized no one was in the cave with her. She almost started screaming as she pulled back the vines covering the cave entrance. Then she saw her savior washing her son and himself in the stream, hearing the giggles her son was making—something she had never heard him do before.

Relief washed over her, and she watched them for a moment, her heart swelling with gratitude and a newfound sense of hope. Her son looked so happy, his laughter echoing through the morning air. She stepped out of the cave, feeling the warmth of the early sun on her skin, and approached them with a smile.

As she got closer, she saw her savior gently washing the grime and soot from her son's small body. He was giggling as his head was dunked just enough to get it wet, and his savior's hands scrubbed his hair clean. Her son looked up with the biggest grin, clearly enjoying the experience.

"Good morning," she said softly, her voice filled with warmth. "Thank you for taking care of him." "It's my pleasure. He is just as much my responsibility as he is yours now," I said, smiling at her.

She saw our pile of dirty clothes and decided to shed hers as well. She stepped into the stream, washing off the grime and soot. I picked up her son, and we sat down on the rocks lining the stream's bed to dry off, giving her space to wash herself.

As she cleansed herself in the cool water, her son and I watched the sunlight dance on the rippling surface. His giggles continued, a sound of pure joy that filled the morning air. It was a moment of peace and normalcy, a brief respite from the chaos they had fled.

After she finished washing, she sat by her son, and we let the sun dry off our bodies. I took our clothes and spread them in the water, and she handed me some bigger stones to hold them in place so the stream wouldn't carry them away. We let the stream wash our clothes, watching as the water flowed over them, carrying away the grime of our journey.

After a while, we both collected our wet clothes, wrung them out, and laid them on the rocks to dry. The sun was warm, and the gentle breeze added to the sense of peace. We sat together, enjoying the quiet moment, knowing that we had found a temporary sanctuary.

She looks at me while we are back sitting together, and she says, "Thank you," her voice barely above a whisper, "for everything you are doing for us."

No, I must thank you for trusting me and following me. I know it was a rough decision, not knowing what could happen. She nods to him, her eyes filled with tears; she realizes that I risked everything to not only save myself but also to save them.

We three sat there on the rocks, our bodies glistening clean in the sunlight, with the worries about what was going on now behind us. The sound of the stream, the birds, and the wildlife around us created a peaceful atmosphere.

We looked at each other, and she nestled her head on my shoulder; somehow, love was blossoming. She smiled and couldn't help but feel a sense of intimacy and vulnerability being so close to me. We both felt that love had invaded us and a connection was being formed. I looked down at her and told her how grateful I was to have her and her son sharing it with me. "I agree," she said. "This love is the purest form."

We gathered up our dried cloths, and after we finished getting dressed, she took her son back inside the cave. I grabbed my spear and blade, then headed to forage for something to eat.

I ventured into the forest, spear and blade in hand, ready to forage for food. The afternoon sun filtered through the canopy, casting dappled light on the forest floor. The air was fresh, filled with the scent of pine and earth. I moved quietly, listening for the sounds of wildlife and looking for signs of edible plants.

I started by searching for wild berries. I knew that certain berries, like blackberries and raspberries, were safe to eat and often grew in clusters along the edges of clearings. After a short walk, I found a patch of blackberries, their dark, plump fruits glistening in the sunlight.

Next, I looked for edible greens. I knew that dandelion greens, wild spinach, and nettles were nutritious and relatively easy to find. I spotted a patch of dandelions, their bright yellow flowers standing out against the green foliage.

As I continued my search, I came across a fallen tree with mushrooms growing at its base. I recognized them as chanterelles, a delicious and safe variety.

With my foraging complete, I returned to the stream, my hands full of fresh, wild food. I felt a sense of accomplishment and relief, knowing that we would have a nourishing meal to sustain us. I washed the berries and greens in the cool water, then headed back to the cave to share my findings with Tylorin and her son.

I returned to the cave with my hands full of fresh, wild food. Tylorin looked up as I entered, her eyes lighting up at the sight of the berries, greens, and mushrooms.

"Look what I found," I said, laying the food out on a flat rock. "We have blackberries, dandelion greens, and chanterelle mushrooms."

Tylorin's son crawled over, his curiosity piqued by the colorful berries. He reached out and grabbed a handful, stuffing them into his mouth with a delighted giggle. Tylorin smiled, her eyes softening as she watched her son enjoy the fresh food.

"Thank you," she said, her voice filled with gratitude. "This will be a feast compared to what we've had lately."

We shared the food, savoring the fresh, natural flavors. The berries were sweet and juicy, the greens slightly bitter but refreshing, and the mushrooms added a rich, earthy taste. It was a simple meal, but it felt like a banquet after the hardships we had faced.

As we ate, we discussed our next steps. "We need to decide what to do next," I said. "We can't stay here forever, but we need to find a safe place where we can rest and rebuild our strength."

Tylorin nodded. "I agree. We should move cautiously and find a place where we can stay safe. Maybe we can find a village or a secluded area where we can start anew."

"We'll need to gather more supplies and plan our route carefully," I added. "But for now, let's focus on resting and regaining our strength. We have a long journey ahead of us."

With our plan set, we felt a renewed sense of purpose and determination. The bond between us had grown stronger, and we were ready to face whatever challenges lay ahead.

A month passed, and the cave had become a temporary home for us. The days were filled with a sense of routine and peace, a stark contrast to the chaos we had fled. Tylorin spent her time teaching her son about the forest and its inhabitants, showing him how to interact with the wildlife.

One morning, as the sun filtered through the trees, a group of deer approached the stream. Tylorin knelt down, her son by her side, and began to communicate with the deer in a soft, melodic language. The deer seemed to understand, their ears twitching and eyes watching her intently.

I watched from a distance, fascinated by the interaction. Tylorin's son reached out a small hand, and one of the deer stepped closer, nuzzling his palm. His laughter filled the air—a sound of pure joy.

Tylorin looked up at me and smiled. "They understand us," she explained. "Elves have a special connection with nature. We can communicate with animals and understand their needs and feelings."

I nodded, amazed by the bond she shared with the wildlife. "It's incredible," I said. "I've never seen anything like it."

She stood up and walked over to me, her son following closely. "It's something we learn from a young age," she said. "It's a way to live in harmony with the world around us."

different directions, and she would return to us to explain what she had learned.

One morning, Tylorin returned with a serious expression. "The deer have seen something over the horizon," she said. "They sense that we need to head west, deeper into the mountains. They will lead us."

We quickly gathered our belongings. I had her son riding on my shoulders as we traveled, and we took turns carrying him, stopping every now and then to rest. Our provisions were becoming low; food and drink were down to just a handful, and we had been traveling for days.

The journey was arduous, but the deer's guidance gave us hope. They led us through dense forests and over rocky terrain, always staying just within sight. Their presence was a comforting reminder that we were not alone.

As we walked, Tylorin and I discussed our plans. "We need to find a place where we can replenish our supplies," I said. "A stream or a small village, perhaps."

Tylorin nodded. "The deer mentioned a valley up ahead. They said it has fresh water and plenty of food. We should aim to reach it by nightfall."

We pressed on, driven by the promise of a safe haven. The sun was beginning to set when we finally reached the valley. It was a beautiful, secluded spot with a clear stream running through it and an abundance of wild plants and berries.

"We'll set up camp here," I said, relief evident in my voice. "This place will give us the chance to rest and gather what we need."

Tylorin smiled, her eyes reflecting the same relief. "Thank you," she said softly. "For everything."

We set up a small camp, using the skills we had learned during our time in the cave. As night fell, we sat by the stream, grateful for the deer's guidance.

Morning sun rose up and I gathered some berries and drank some water and followed the stream northward for a little bit, Its when I saw threw the overgrown bushes a chimney, Nestled among the trees, I found an old, abandoned cottage. It was close to the clear stream and surrounded by wild plants and berries. The cottage looked weathered but sturdy, a relic from a time long past.

"This could be a good place to rest and replenish our supplies," I said, feeling a sense of relief. I headed back to where Tylorin was sleeping, but she was already up, feeding her son. Deer lay around them, almost as if they were guarding them. As I approached, the deer got up and began foraging.

I told Tylorin about my discovery, and we gathered our belongings. We walked around the bend northward, with the deer following us. The forest was alive with the sounds of rustling leaves and distant bird calls. Suddenly, a majestic buck emerged from the under-brush, standing tall and imposing in front of Tylorin. She raised her hand, signaling me to halt as well.

We watched in awe as the deer cautiously moved through the bushes and tall grass, their ears twitching at every sound. "They're making sure no varmints or dangerous critters are lurking about," Tylorin explained, her voice barely above a whisper. The tension in the air was palpable as we waited. Once the area was cleared, the big buck stepped aside, permitting us to enter the clearing and approach the cottage.

This old cottage hadn't seen life for many years, but we claimed it as our new home. Tylorin looked around the dilapidated structure with a mix of excitement and relief. "It's a bit run-down and in need of repair, but it's shelter, and that is all that matters," she said, her voice filled with determination. She set down our belongings and surveyed the room, taking in the old, broken furniture and the cobwebs hanging from the ceiling. Dust motes danced in the shafts of sunlight that pierced through the cracks in the walls. "This will do," she said, a smile spreading across her face, her eyes sparkling with hope.

"Yes," I agreed with her, feeling a sense of peace wash over me. "We can make this a home, our home, without fear of the world we left behind." As we stood there, the weight of our past seemed to lift, replaced by the promise of a new beginning.

During our time together, we had bonded deeply, realizing that our futures were intertwined. Raising her child, whom I had come to love as my own, solidified our connection. Since the cave experience, our relationship had blossomed into something intimate and profound. Being together meant the world to us, and this cottage, though humble, was a symbol of our resilience and hope.

Tylorin nods, feeling peace and security wash over her. For the first time in a long while, she feels like they have found a place they can truly call their own. She looks at me, her eyes shining with love and gratitude. "Thank you," she says softly, her voice trembling with emotion.

"For being here with me, for making this possible. I don't know what I'd do without you."

I reach out and take her hand, squeezing it gently. "We're in this together," I reply, my voice filled with conviction. "We've come this far, and we'll keep moving forward, no matter what."

We cleaned an area so our son had a safe place to crawl and lay down, then Tylorin and I started tidying up the old cottage. After a while, we went outside and gathered some foliage to fill our empty bellies. We relaxed, knowing we had found our place in this uncertain world. Looking out, we saw our deer friends nesting for the night, a comforting sight that reassured us we were in a safe area.

As the sun dipped below the horizon, casting a warm glow over the clearing, Tylorin picked up our son, cleaned him up, and bundled him so he could sleep. Exhausted from the journey and the cleaning, we laid out our skins on the floor. We cuddled up, holding each other close, and fell asleep in each other's arms, feeling a deep sense of contentment and hope for the future.

Our future as a family still had not been written, but we were bonded by love and commitment to each other. No man nor beast would be able to break our bond. As our family grew, we lived a happy life, cherishing each moment together. The years passed, and we found joy in the simple things, knowing that our love and unity were our greatest strengths. We grew old together, surrounded by the warmth of our family and the peace of our home. And threw the years the wildlife became more as part of our family as we became part of theirs.

www.ingramcontent.com/pod-product-compliance
Lightning Source LLC
Chambersburg PA
CBHW071228140726
47996CB00004B/1527